P9-CLC-103

The Not-So Itty-Bitty Spiders

Read more
Olive & Beatrix
books!

Olive & Beatrix
The Not-So
Itty-Bitty
Spiders

BRANCHES

■SCHOLASTIC
Amy Marie
Stadelmann

Olive & Beatrix
The
Super-Smelly
Moldy Blob

BRANCHES

■SCHOLASTIC
Amy Marie
Stadelmann

The Not-So Itty-Bitty Spiders

by Amy Marie Stadelmann

SCHOLASTIC INC.

For my grandma—thanks for being my very first art teacher!

If you purchased this book without a cover, you should be aware that this book is stolen property. It was reported as "unsold and destroyed" to the publisher, and neither the author nor the publisher has received any payment for this "stripped book."

Copyright © 2015 by Amy Marie Stadelmann

All rights reserved. Published by Scholastic Inc. *Publishers since 1920.*
SCHOLASTIC, BRANCHES, and associated logos are trademarks and/or registered trademarks of Scholastic Inc.

The publisher does not have any control over and does not assume any responsibility for author or third-party websites and their content.

No part of this publication may be reproduced, stored in a retrieval system, or transmitted in any form or by any means, electronic, mechanical, photocopying, recording, or otherwise, without written permission of the publisher. For information regarding permission, write to Scholastic Inc., Attention: Permissions Department, 557 Broadway, New York, NY 10012.

This book is a work of fiction. Names, characters, places, and incidents are either the product of the author's imagination or are used fictitiously, and any resemblance to actual persons, living or dead, business establishments, events, or locales is entirely coincidental.

Library of Congress Cataloging-in-Publication Data
The Not-So Itty-Bitty Spiders / by Amy Marie Stadelmann.
pages cm. — (Olive & Beatrix ; #1)
Summary: Beatrix is a witch, but her twin sister Olive is not, and when Beatrix plays one trick too many on Olive and their classmate Eddie the two decide to get back at her with a bucket of garden spiders—but when the spiders get into a growing potion and turn into giant spiders the three children have to work together to save their town.
ISBN 0-545-81480-4 (pbk.) — ISBN 0-545-81481-2 (hardcover) —
ISBN 0-545-81482-0 (ebook) — ISBN 0-545-81483-9 (eba ebook) 1. Witches—Juvenile fiction. 2. Twins—Juvenile fiction. 3. Sisters—Juvenile fiction. 4. Spiders—Juvenile fiction. 5. Practical jokes—Juvenile fiction. 6. Magic—Juvenile fiction. [1. Witches—Fiction. 2. Twins—Fiction. 3. Sisters—Fiction. 4. Spiders—Fiction. 5. Magic—Fiction.]
I. Title.
PZ7.1.S72No 2015
[E]—dc23
2014041880

ISBN 978-0-545-81481-2 (hardcover) / ISBN 978-0-545-81480-5 (paperback)

10 9 8 7 6 5 4 3 2 1   15 16 17 18 19/0

Printed in China
First edition, September 2015
Edited by Katie Carella
Book design by Becky James

Table of Contents

Not a Witch at All

Hi! My name is Olive. And this is my sister, Beatrix. We're twins!

Me

Beatrix

Beatrix may look like an ordinary girl, but she's not. She is a witch.

Head full of tricks

Fingers that make magic

Talking pet pig

You may call me Sir Houston.

I may also look like an ordinary girl. That's because I am. I'm not a witch at all.

Head full of smarts

Fingers that just snap

Non-talking pet bugs

3

Beatrix was born exactly at midnight during a full moon. That is what makes her a witch.

I was born two minutes later, like a regular, boring baby.

We live in the quiet town of Juniper Hollows. Our house is in between Berry Hill Park and the Dark Woods.

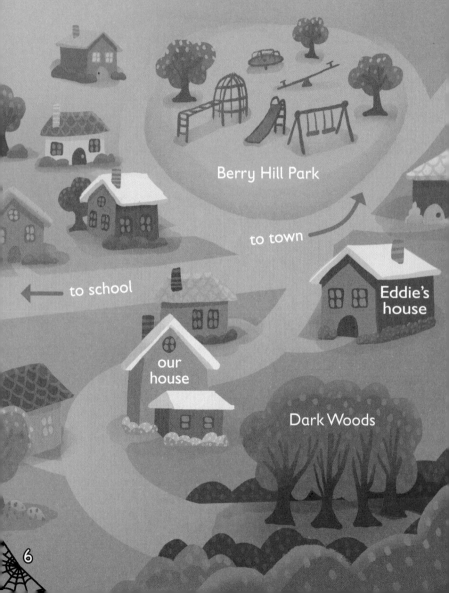

Berry Hill Park

to town

to school

Eddie's house

our house

Dark Woods

This is Eddie. He lives next door, and he is my best friend.

Eddie

Just like me, Eddie loves science. He also loves to make up songs about everything!

Baking soda and vinegar are a tricky pair! Mix them together for some real stinky, fizzy air!

VINEGAR

BAKING SODA

7

Eddie and I do all sorts of important science projects. But Beatrix is always playing tricks on us!

She casts floating spells.

She sneak-attacks on her broom.

So much for space travel.

Sigh.

And she even does sneaky sneezing hexes!

ACHOO!

Bravo, Miss Beatrix.

Eddie and I have had enough. Today, we are going to play a trick on Beatrix.

I know exactly what we'll do.

Itty-Bitty Spiders

If there is one thing my sister is afraid of, it's spiders. So Eddie and I collected spiders from the garden. We were going to need <u>a lot</u> of them.

I've never met a witch who's afraid of spiders.

You've never met a witch other than Beatrix.

Good point.

We collected as many spiders as we could find. Then we poured them into a bucket. I balanced the bucket over Beatrix's door.

Bea is going to freak out!

Yes! Now she'll know what it feels like to be tricked!

To trick a witch is a risky trick.

Eddie and I hid. We couldn't wait to see Beatrix's face when all those spiders came tumbling out!

Beatrix never saw it coming.

Well, I told Hilda, if you curse him, he'll never sit with you at lun—

Our trick worked perfectly! My sister was completely covered in teeny-tiny, itty-bitty spiders!

Eddie and I high-fived. Just then, there was a loud crash from inside Beatrix's room.

Down Came the Blame

The biggest, hairiest, scariest spider
<u>EVER</u> stood in Beatrix's doorway!

And there were more where that one
came from . . .

Eddie pointed to the window. We had been so busy arguing that we didn't see the spiders make their escape. Now we had an even <u>bigger</u> problem.

We looked out the window . . .

Beatrix was right: The spiders really were having a wild time.

They were making all kinds of messes!

They weeded the garden!

They climbed to new heights!

They even had a fashion show!

Things were not looking good for Juniper Hollows. Eddie's and my little trick had turned into a <u>huge</u> disaster.

We were going to need Beatrix's help to put things right. We were going to need magic.

Eight-Legged Beasts

Beatrix got to work on her shrinking potion while Eddie and I <u>tried</u> to keep an eye on the giant spiders.

Come ON, Bea! The spiders are on the move! We need that potion now!

I've got it! But there's only enough for us to use it once. We'll need to get all of the spiders in one group.

We planned to shrink these spiders down to their normal size. But first, we had to find them. And for that, we needed the proper gear.

A Super-Duper Spider-Sucker!

A rainmaker!

A spider-proof hat!

A pig!

Why me?

And, of course, extra wands.

It was time for a spider hunt.

The giant spider grabbed Eddie right up, off the ground.

eee?!

GAH!

I said "Go to sleep"! Not "Sweep me off my feet"!

Quick as a flash, Beatrix pulled out her wand and zapped the spider! It scurried away.

ZAP!

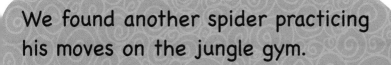

We found another spider practicing his moves on the jungle gym.

Okay! Time to use our Super-Duper Spider-Sucker!

Otherwise known as a vacuum.

When Eddie doesn't know what else to do, he sings.

The itsy-bitsy spider climbed up the waterspout. Down came the rain and washed the spider out. Out came—

Wait. Did you say <u>rain</u>, Eddie?

That's it! We'll wash the spiders away! Bea, can you make it rain?

Step aside, dull skulls!

With a swish of her wand, Beatrix started to say a spell.

39

The rain fell and fell. But the spiders did not get washed away. They actually seemed to enjoy the shower.

I guess rain only works on itsy-bitsy spiders ...

What's for Lunch?

Why didn't I think of this sooner?

Haven't you noticed that they all seem to be going somewhere?

Beatrix and Eddie looked around.

The spiders were gone.

The spiders must be looking for food!

And of course they don't want to eat us. Tiny spiders eat bugs, so giant ones do, too. Obviously.

Beatrix, Eddie, and I put our heads together.

So spiders eat bugs.

And <u>giant</u> spiders eat LOTS of bugs . . .

Into the Woods

My biggest fear in the whole wide world is the dark. And here we were, walking right into the darkest place of all: the Dark Woods.

Come ON, Olive!

We headed into the woods. Darkness was everywhere! Beatrix and Eddie tried to tell me that I had nothing to be afraid of.

Don't be afraid of the dark, my friend!
All your fears are nothing but pretend!
The dark is shy and it hides from view . . .
The dark is, in fact, afraid of you!

I'm not sure that's true . . .

Beatrix used her magic wand to light the way.

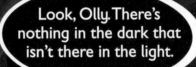

Look, Olly. There's nothing in the dark that isn't there in the light.

As we walked, I began to feel better. The Dark Woods weren't as scary as I had imagined. And I even started to feel a bit brave!

Fearless explorer Olive the Mighty coming through!

Sure enough, we soon found the giant spiders. They were all together—on one giant, sparkling web.

It's beautiful!

It's horrible.

It's sticky.

That's what I call a spiderweb!

Now that the spiders were finally all in one place, we needed to shrink them down to their original size. But then, one of the spiders spotted us.

Suddenly, thousands of giant-spider eyes looked out at us from the dark.

GULP! Maybe giant spiders don't eat <u>bugs</u> after all!

We needed to move fast!

Beatrix, Eddie, and I returned the itty-bitty spiders to the garden.

Then we stood up. And we looked around Juniper Hollows.

The giant spiders had made a truly giant mess! Beatrix, Eddie, and I got to work.

And that's the story of how we almost destroyed—but then saved—the day from giant spiders.

Amy Marie Stadelmann

Amy did not grow up with a sister who was a witch, or with a talking pig. But she did grow up with a <u>very</u> active imagination! She often imagined that she had magical powers and could talk to animals. Like Olive, Amy loves reading and is curious about the world around her. And, like Beatrix, she is horribly afraid of spiders! Amy lives in Brooklyn, New York, with a non-talking dog. Olive & Beatrix is her first children's book series.

Olive & Beatrix

Questions and Activities!

Why is only <u>one</u> of the twins a witch?

How does Olive and Eddie's trick on Beatrix turn into a big, hairy, scary problem?

Write words and draw pictures to describe how Olive, Beatrix, and Eddie finally shrink and capture the spiders!

Do you think Olive and Eddie should have played the trick on Beatrix? Why or why not?

Look at the words and pictures on pages 68 and 69. What is the meaning of the words <u>revive</u> and <u>replace</u>? What does the prefix <u>re</u>- mean?